# THEY TAUGHT US WRONG

## THE FUTURE NIGHT STALKERS

### M. L. BUCHMAN

Buchman Bookworks

M.L. Buchman is guaranteed to get me lost in a good story.

— THE READING CAFE, WAY OF<br>THE WARRIOR: NSDQ

I love Buchman's writing. His vivid descriptions bring everything to life in an unforgettable way.

— PURE JONEL, HOT POINT

# Other works by M. L. Buchman:

M are Tranquillitatis my ass!

Go ahead. Thrash some Duster bastard over Luna's northeastern Nearside. Make him eat death slow and painful.

Then, after you've won, after his ass is going down hard, his drive goes nova. It kicks out an electromagnetic pulse so hard that it cooks your ship, too. You dump out two klicks up and watch your ship punch a new crater close beside his.

See how you feel about that shit.

Scary as hell ride down. The EMP had cooked my suit's electronics as well. I had to handle the landing retros manually. Ran out of fuel a few dozen meters up—damn glad this was Luna grav and not Earth's unforgiving full-g. Felt the leg go when I hit, but I was down and the suit was intact for all the good it did me.

Welcome to the fucking Sea of Tranquility.

The Duster's ship had gone as bright as a second sun, before it piled into the inside cliff face of Cauchy Crater, less than a dozen klicks away. Instead of acting like a beacon shouting "Come save my ass," the crater had funneled all that light into a beam that was crossing nobody's path—not Earth, not some off-track freighter. Like a rifle shot due north, it was going straight up. Some dipwad alien scientist sitting on the North Star four hundred years from now might scratch himself and wonder what that tiny fleck of brightness could be, but I wasn't counting on it.

As if the busted leg hadn't just stamped 'Paid' on my ticket, my Army training kicked in and I checked my suit. Dead. H2 and oxy recyc had enough mechanical fail-safes to give me something to drink and breath for now. All I could do was hope the suit blocked the rads of the reactor burst, because the dosimeter readout had cooked along with the rest of my electronics. No dosimeter, no radio, no readouts on how much longer I'd have before even the recyc couldn't save me. Not even a beacon in case someone did come looking.

I unclipped my **RACR** and fired a shot at a likely rock. The Recoilless Army Combat Rifle didn't recoil, but it didn't shatter the rock either. Three kilos of dead plastic and fried electronics.

I slammed a hypo through my suit leg, trying not to scream at the jarring to my broken bone. The cold clarity of the meds washed through me and the limb went blessedly numb.

The Army taught us a whole lot about how to survive in hard places. Zero atmo and the one-sixth g of Luna's surface wasn't anything new in the manual. Sitting in a white-gray camo suit at the bottom of a three-klick deep crater four hundred kilometers from the next nearest piece of humanity without even a signal flare? Not so much.

Walking that distance was in range, if my leg hadn't decided to take leave without permission. Didn't really matter; without the nav gear, I didn't stand a chance of finding a specific point four hundred klicks away. There wasn't shit at the old Apollo 17 site anyway except scrap—Chinese had gotten pissed half a century back, when there was still a China, and dropped a ten-thousand kilo shrapnel head right at ground zero. Shock-wave munitions—concussers—didn't work in zero atmo, but the shrap-heads never left anything bigger than a boot sole behind, not for a long way round. The Chinese blew out the museum, the historic lander and buggy, and about three hundred tourists—all done back before this shit war when there were still tourists.

Army trainers had pounded a lot into my thick skull. Not a single piece of which was going to salvage this screwed-up mess. No impossible engineering feat sprouting from my grunt brain. No "just lean into the fucking traces, man, and grunt it out" solution. Even in one-sixth g I wasn't going to hop one-legged for four hundred kilometers to nowhere. No miracles—not out here.

I was dead; I knew that. But I was no cracker. I'd keep my helmet closed and hold on for every second I had.

Army did a whole lot of mental training. Will to survive was high on their list. But how to turn fear into something useful was the big one—useful to them anyway.

*You'll be afraid. Don't care who you are, you'll be shitting your pants when you're in it.*

A lot they knew. Why didn't the psychs ever actually fly a mission? Too goddamn scared was my guess.

They didn't get that fear came *before* the mission. During the fight, there was only time for adrenaline and survival.

*You've got to turn that fear. Turn it to anger! Turn it to rage! Turn it to winning the battle!*

Fuckin' psychs.

We did what they told us. Afraid of something? *Attack it!* Except the fear came before the mission—we turned it anyway. We'd beat on each other in the ready room, throwing "friendly" punches that would level a grunt if they weren't as wound up on adrenaline as the next jock. We'd *start* the flight with bruises purpling and fear-eating grins plastered on our faces. Yeah, we had the old turn-fear-into-rage routine nailed.

Fear when you went down was different kind of thing. I'd beaten the odds about three hundred-to-one by surviving. Couldn't get that kind of help in a poker game, but I had the luck now for all the good it was doing.

No way to rescue myself and no one looking for me here.

Zara had eaten it at the far end of Mare Fecunditatis—Sea of Fertility. *Shit!* She'd been the best partner I'd ever had in flight or in the sack. New Army thinking—fighting partners who were also fucking partners.

*Heightened wingman bond. Subjects more likely to go to extreme measures to defend their sleep mate.*

"Sleep mate." Lame-ass psychs—like that even began to cover it.

Zara had rocked. Better than anyone, even before the Army and their psychs got their claws in me. Zara and I had talked about rooting down together when our tours were up. Meant it, too. It hadn't been some feebs' pillow talk; we'd meant it right down to our boots.

Yeah, stamp 'Paid' on that one, too.

You want terror, you fuckin' psychs? Not fear, but unholy, mind-numbing, shit-in-your-suit terror? You watch a renegade Duster zero in on your wingmate when your thrust vector is going the other way and there isn't squat you can do about it. That'll teach you terror.

But I'd turned it. Yes I did. I turned that terror into one flaming, searing, ball-busting tower of pissed-as-hell fighter-jock rage. Rather than just killing him and going home alive, I took that Duster apart one piece at a time. I moved in close and hurt him and kept on hurting him. No kill—just pain.

When I finally let the bastard die—when he'd crisscrossed a thousand kilometers of Luna trying to get away but knowing he was going to burn in hell—I got close enough to see him right through his canopy. Almost close enough to hear his final scream despite the gap of empty space between us.

But he'd kept that one last trick up his sleeve.

When his engine blew, it fucking went EMP, cooking all my circuits.

And down I went, too.

I tried to spot the new craters our two ships had punched—side-by-side holes a kilometer up Cauchy's side.

Not even a hint. It was night and only cold Earthshine lit that section of crater wall. Earthshine would never reach me here at the bottom of Cauchy's icy deep. Even sunrise—still a week away—would never reach me.

The ships had hit in the steepest part of the rim's cliff. They'd probably triggered a rockfall to bury any trace. Only evidence left was me.

Some day, a thousand years from now, some geologist would stumble on my camouflaged suit—almost the same color as the soil and lightly dusted with micrometeorites. He'd have to look up my suit design in some historical database to figure out what century I'd been fucked by. My personal recorder was cooked, so no record there. No pad or pen, so I couldn't even leave him a goddamn note. I considered scrabbling a long message in the Lunar dust; it would last for centuries.

Then, like some lovesick recruit, I simply scribed two first names—mine and Zara's. It wouldn't mean anything to anyone but me, but I liked seeing it there.

She'd taught me joy in war. She'd trained me, far more thoroughly than the psychs, that there were emotions other than fear and rage—even Army victory celebrations weren't joy; they were rage thinly disguised as triumph.

More important than joy, Zara had taught me hope. Hope of one day seeing a girl with her long hair floating behind as she raced down the corridors of Tycho City. Of a boy with her mother's light eyes watching a ball bounce in one-sixth g and seeing nothing strange because he'd never been to a full-g planet.

The recyc ran out. I felt the tightness growing in my chest. Oxy-dep setting in. I knew my training. From when I could truly feel it—not some fear or panic reaction, but really feel it—I would have only moments before it killed me. They'd learned that the slow bleed-out of oxygen depravation led to unpredictable panic attacks, bad news in armed soldiers with hell-bent rage burning in their guts. So the recyc ran at a hundred percent until it was gone. The air in the suit was good for three more thinning breaths, maybe four, then I'm done.

One final look at the stars Zara and I had dreamed beneath.

Lying here in my last moments, I learned a new fear.

One that the goddamn psychs would never be able to understand no matter how I tried to explain. It wasn't a fear born of rage or vengeance or honor. It was born of something they could never know—weren't capable of knowing. Weren't worthy of.

My fear, Zara? The one thing that shrivels me? The one thing I can't turn into soothing, familiar rage?

It's that the woman who taught me to love so deeply might not be there waiting for me when I cross over.

# THE NARA REACTION (EXCERPT)

## A TALE OF THE APOCALYPSE

"**S**o, I'm dead, am I?"

It was perfect. James Wirden's voice started with all the power one would expect from the World Premier, but it ended the most delicious twist of uncertainty. Bryce looked down at the nearly empty champagne glass in James' hand.

"Yes, sad for you, but true. Poisoned, if you must know. By me."

"And you dare to tell me this?" Such indignation from such a small man. He turned toward the guards, but Bryce clamped a friendly hand upon his shoulder to belay the movement. Not that it mattered, all of the guards along the line of French doors were his hand-picked staff. The bright lights from within cast their tall shadows across the stone terrace pushing back the edge of the Bermudan night. His men would stop any stragglers from the party, not that any would dare interrupt when the Premier and his mighty right-hand man were in conference. But no point in misplacing trust when one staged a coup.

"One of the many things you never properly appreciated, James, is the wonders of modern genetics. There is a tiny little code-alterer running through your system even as we speak. Your genetic code is even now shifting at an exquisitely subtle level. When you have a massive stroke in three days, none shall grieve as much as your lieutenant. None shall take power with as much trepidation as your Right Hand." A nickname Bryce had carefully cultivated for years. Who better to be named to power than the man who knew the Premier's every intent?

The man struggled against his grasp just as pointlessly as a worm evading a short future pithed upon the hook that would send it into the fish's belly. Bryce took the champagne glass from James' nerveless hand and tipped the dregs over the broad stone seawall to splash into the eager waves below. Soon, he promised them, soon you may swallow this useless chattel as well.

The Premier's pale face twisted in such pain that for a moment Bryce feared the stroke would come too soon. He didn't have everything in place yet. Of course, he could compensate, but having the man die in his arms would not look good at all to the World Economic Council.

"You must remember to breathe, my good leader.

Besides, in another few minutes you will remember none of this. Another wonder of genetics research you so despise is the revelation of how memories are stored. Your memory of these moments will shortly be erased. And when you pass on in three day's time, your Right Hand will be there, the Premier-to-be, Bryce Randall Stevens, Sr."

James patted at the beads of sweat on his brow with his small hand as he looked up at Bryce. He always backed up when they spoke so that he didn't have to crane his neck, but Bryce kept him in his place this time. The music surged through the open doors onto the broad patio. The orchestra had come back precisely on schedule drawing everyone's attention inward. He didn't want any to think his conversation with the Premier took overlong if the drug didn't take effect as planned. Of course he knew it would, it had worked perfectly on the man who'd engineered it for him.

"Do you hate me so?"

"Stupid man, what does hate have to do with anything? You're weak, James. Always were. If I hadn't pulled every single string over the last four decades, Parvati and her temple of democratic fairness would still be in power. I have used you, because you are far more presentable than I. No one expects a small, rotund man to be vicious. Therefore, there were no curious eyes as I did what you were too weak to do behind the scenes. But now you are beginning to interfere. You should never have nuked Auckland."

The little man sputtered. "I had to Bryce. You and your damned gene labs. There is a reason we outlawed that horrible knowledge. We did it. You and I. Together. When I found you were dabbling in that dark road to hell, of course I had to blow it out of existence."

"Too little, too late, James. Do you think I'd have let you drop those bombs if I wasn't ready? All you did for me was a little convenient housecleaning." Actually he'd barely gotten the chief scientists and the data clear. Less than an hour warning had let him salvage only the most essential elements. But the continuing research on the uses of the Second Human Genome Mapping Project lived on, even if the researchers families hadn't. And he'd gotten to look like the hero to the ones he had saved.

The blow of his failure took the fight out of the Premier. Bryce gave James' shoulder a jovial shake in show for any who might be watching.

"On December 24th, three days after this birthday party, lovingly thrown by your second-in-command, I shall mourn at your side. I shall cancel Christmas throughout the planet. It shall be a splendid funeral. And by the New Year, the World Economic Council will place me in command and then things shall really start to move."

James' little eyes squinted up at him for a long

moment before turning to look out at the restless sea. He hung onto the rough seawall to keep from being toppled by the gentle night breeze and stared toward the dark waves.

"They will suspect you."

"There will be no proof. The last of the drug has just been dribbled into the sea. The change to your genetic code has already been registered in your electronic medical records, by a fine hacker who has, alas, suffered a memory loss due to some bad fish he ate. Very bad fish. You don't maintain paper files, so I'm safe."

Bryce leaned down to watch his face, but James was turned toward the night and he was totally in shadow. There was a long hesitation, then a twitch of his shoulders that Bryce could feel beneath his hand.

"But I do. I was most careful."

Not careful enough, old friend. He knew when James' was lying. It was for this that Bryce had risked telling him of his own death. The man was so naive that he hadn't banked hard copies against his future. So, Bryce's plan was going to go off without a hitch.

The Premier hung his head and his voice was a mere whisper against the susurration of the surf on the rocky cliffs below.

"What about my wife?"

Bryce glanced back to the surging dance floor. What an odd final question to ask before certain death. Given a chance, what would be his last request? Not about some woman, that was for certain. Though if ever there was one…

Even through the crowd Celia Wirden stood out. Her fountain of white-blond hair and the slender body beneath, shimmeringly not revealed by her gown of midnight-blue silk, did everything to distract from the brilliant mind that hid behind those green eyes.

The three of them had plotted together since they were young. They had thrown Parvati out of power and when it came time to choose, Bryce had forced the milquetoast James to puppet the Premiership for him. And the Premier needed a First Lady. A fine and elegant First Lady she had made. Perhaps it was time to take that gift back.

"She'll be taken care of, James. You don't need to fear for that."

James' shoulders squared slowly as the man looked a last time at the dark Atlantic. He took up his empty champagne glass from the seawall.

"Well, old friend. Seems that I am dry. Shall we go get a refill?"

"I am right beside you to the end of your days, James."

"Long may that be."

Bryce completed their old code, "Long indeed."

At the French doors, he checked James one last time. But he was filled with a bonhomie that even the finest politician couldn't invent. When he refilled the same glass and drank from it, Bryce knew the memory of the last few minutes was safely gone.

James was wrapped up into the flow of the crowd as Bryce waited upon the threshold. The broad squares of alternating black and white marble spread across the room before him like a grand chess board. The sycophants rushed to make what they could of the moment, shuffling like mad pawns, the tuxedoed livery of the government descended upon the wrong man. The short stature of the largest pawn of them all disappeared from view. Bryce would keep a close eye upon him, but not too close. Nothing must seem out of the ordinary.

He scanned the room. The ladies, those dragged forward by their men, and those abandoned in the sudden rush toward the Premier, glittered about. Their 1920s flapper costumes revealing both the wondrous and the corpulent with an equal lack of sympathy. But they too were all either carefully watching the rush to the Premier, or carefully not watching.

There were just four who were watching the Premier's Right Hand instead. His Captain of the guard, meticulous in his waiter's outfit, was nonchalantly poised to strike from his corner like a steadfast rook. The general commander of the World Economic Council's forces waited like the good knight he was, not obviously aligned, yet always prepared to offer surprise support from unexpected quarters.

Celia Wirden glittered like the queen that she was. The tight silk revealed a mature woman who had grown into her body the way a yacht grows into a World Cup racer. Her movements could light fire without ever striking a match.

His body responded from the memory of that one tryst three decades gone, the same night he'd sent her to become James' first lady. Her green eyes assessed him carefully from her position far across the room near the small orchestra. A chandelier blossomed above her in a font of crystal as if it had bloomed for her alone.

And off to the side, behind the piano, hid a single junior pawn. Without even the boy being aware, Bryce had been moving him across the board, square by careful square. Perhaps it was time to move the lad one step closer to the far side of the board, where he too would become powerful. Together, many things could be achieved. He would kill the king, take the queen, and create a prince.

Yes. It was time for the next move.

A **hand descended out** of the darkness and landed on Ri's shoulder. She knew the hand instantly. Only Tinnai, of the whole cadre, dared touch her without warning. Others had learned all too well of her hair-trigger reflexes.

"I'm ready, Tinnai." Ri kept her young girl's voice at a barest whisper.

Tinnai's nod was more felt than seen in the darkness. Taking her hand, the cadre leader placed something heavy in it. A pipe. The pipe! Tinnai had been sharpening it for weeks on the concrete. The constant grinding noise now a part of everyone's dreams. The point shone wickedly. Even in the overcast, moonless night, she could see the glimmer of the steel-bright edge. It was almost as long as she was tall. A fearsome weapon.

"Tonight. You guide us." And then, impossibly,

Tinnai bowed to her. A shadow upon shadow. Bowed deeply. Honor and respect from the cadre leader. If Ri had still been a young one, she'd have started to cry. But not tonight. Tonight, Tancho Cadre's fate lay in her hands. There had never been a more important fight. And it was hers to lead.

She returned the leader's bow, hefted the pipe to the center of balance, the surface rust rough against her palm, and turned to face along the sidewalk. The cracked concrete beneath her bare feet made her feel more stable. She tried to breathe slowly and shallowly so that the vapor that escaped her mouth into the freezing air would be even less visible in the night.

Tinnai rested her hand on Ri's shoulder. In moments the signal passed up the line just as they'd rehearsed. A squeezed shoulder, from girl to girl up the entire line until Tinnai's hand squeezed Ri's and they were ready to go.

Tonight she didn't run with a small group of hunters. Tonight, the entire cadre hunted the streets of Nara together. Tancho Cadre. The Fighting Cranes. They owned this night. Nineteen girls strong from four to sixteen years old. In the last city of Japan. Maybe the last one on Earth.

She touched the rough brick of the old wall beside her to make sure of her direction and moved forward. Each crack in the sidewalk an old friend. Walked but twice in a month of planning, once at the beginning to learn, and yesterday to confirm the memory she'd spent four long weeks honing until it sang as a part of her blood.

Fifty-four paces before she reached out again and exactly touched the corner of the brick wall. Her finger traced the small pocket made by a missing chip at exactly the height of her elbow.

She turned right and began a new count. The cadre followed in carefully rehearsed lockstep. The air so cold it had little smell. When it blew from the north, the scent of snow and mountains sometimes clawed into Nara. From the south, it smelled of the sea. From the east was the worst. The smell of cooking, of actual food occasionally rose from Daibutsu-den cadre or from the dark mystery of Nara-ken park. But not tonight. Tonight the air hung still and silent, the wind but another creature holding its breath in the dark.

At fourteen steps, a scuffle by her foot then a squeak as a rat scurried off.

Ri counted to fifty.

All was silent.

She counted to a hundred.

Still nothing.

Fourteen. Her foot had been raised for fifteen. She continued her count and the cadre followed in perfect silence.

At thirty-two she reached out her right hand again and traced the vertical line of the Yen symbol on the steel plaque beside the bank's missing door. She'd asked Tinnai, but no one knew what it meant, only what it was called and that it had been holy.

She turned left and headed across the invisible street toward tonight's target, the one they'd been training to attack for nearly three months. The bookstore lay three and seventeen and two paces ahead.

One. Two. Three. At the curb, she lifted her shoulder high to warn of a change underfoot then stepped off the curb. Weeks of practicing "Follow the Elder" wearing blindfolds paid off. Tinnai's hand shifted as the message passed shoulder to hand down the line of nineteen girls.

Tinnai had berated her for her risks this afternoon. She'd cleared a narrow path through the debris on the street. A little girl, she stood small, even for a ten-year-old, chasing a pretend playmate up and down the street. Hawk Cadre's guards had watched her with disdain. They'd made a fatal mistake and left the silly little girl alone. For once Ri was glad of her small size. In just four heart-stopping passages up and down the street, she'd managed to confirm her practiced distances and to clear tonight's path for the cadre.

She'd had to do it. Rani was clumsy. She couldn't even do the simplest obstacles in the dark without messing up. She didn't cry out after the first hunt she'd ruined. But tonight a stumble, even a scuffed foot, and the whole cadre might go down.

And Tinnai would be far angrier if she knew that Ri had entered the tunnels of the Zenbu beneath the store. A terrible risk, but there she had locked the basement door of the bookstore from the outside, blocking escape. A risk that would cause her nightmares for many nights, if there were more nights.

Seventeen steps, she raised her shoulder and stepped up onto the opposite curb. Only there was no crack in the concrete beneath her bare foot.

Think! Had she veered left or right in the crossing?

She started to slide a foot to the right, searching the surface slick with the night's frost when she heard it. A rattle of teeth.

The sacrificial shivering outside the bolthole. The bookstore's only entry, a knee-high, circular hole. The sacrificial huddled against it for warmth, kept from running away by the chain about his ankle.

She shifted left a half step, felt the concrete crack beneath her foot, took two steps and kicked out. High and hard. Crushing the sacrificial's throat before he could cry out his warning. Leaning in and up at the end of the kick, his neck let go as only a break could cause.

He flopped sideways and Tinnai dove past her into the bolthole. The entire cadre flowed in like a single, long, gutter snake.

Ri ducked through last. By the time she entered,

Tancho Cadre flew forward in full motion through the store. The sacrificial's chainkeeper had no more throat to cry with than the one he'd held captive. A knife slash had left only the ability to stare wide-eyed as he bled out. Firelight flickered from the back of the store, the towering bookcases dark silhouettes.

Some of the cadre ran down the aisles. Others had vaulted onto the cases and ran along the tops leaping over gaps at the aisles. At the back of the store, they were only beginning to suspect an attack in full flight. When the ground team met resistance from the Hawks, the high runners fell upon them from above like deadly rain, their long dark hair streaming out behind them.

Ri raced toward the back of the store. Tinnai and Ninka, Tancho's best hunter, were in pitched battle with a pair of boys armed with clubs. Then two more joined in, racing up from what must be the cellar. Stopped by the door Ri had locked against them.

Now they were coming up the stairs behind Tinnai. Perhaps she should have left the door unlocked so that they could escape if they survived the tunnels of the Zenbu. But a free Hawk could seek revenge.

With a cry, "Behind you!" she swung her pipe at the head of one of the attackers. The weight of it carried it so far into his skull she had trouble freeing it. As he collapsed, the man in front of Tinnai also went down. Even as he died, he lacerated her right arm and it dangled suddenly limp.

Her knife dropped and she dove to grab it with her other hand. But her recovery roll was wrong due to her injured arm. Blood was a sharp edge to the scent of night, the smoke from the firepit stung her eyes.

The Hawk Cadre's leader faced Tinnai. He was man-tall, his chin scraggly with a thin growth of whiskers. His companion fully engaged Ninka, she could do nothing to help. With a feral smile, the leader brandished the longest knife Ri had ever seen. Tinnai was in danger.

Ri charged. No cry. Nor stealth. Nor thought. She brushed by Tinnai's elbow and drove the pipe into the leader's chest. The sharpened, shining point punched a hole right into him, only stopped by the bookcase he staggered against.

His knife didn't drop, but he didn't raise it either. In surprise, he looked down to inspect the pipe protruding from his chest. Then he looked at Ri, just as his heart's blood, black in the dim firelight, gushed out the open end of the pipe and sprayed all over her. The heat spread through her clothes and burned against her chilled skin. He toppled silently to the side like a stray leaf on the still winter air.

Tinnai hamstrung Ninka's attacker and a moment later, Ninka finished him off.

The bookstore was silent. No more fighting. No shouts.

Tinnai called roll. Two didn't answer. Little Rani had killed one Hawk who'd then landed on her and knocked her out against a bookcase. She'd have a good bump for a while, but no worse. Melna was found with a knife between her breasts, but three lay dead around her. An honorable death.

They all turned their attention to the towering bookcases.

Books. Books beyond counting. In the flickering firelight another floor could be seen with more shelves.

"So many books," Ninka breathed into the warm night air inside the bookstore. "We have enough heat for a dozen winters!"

---

RI AWOKE in the golden glow of morning light. And shivered. The fire had died during the night into a blackened firepit and the winter cold bit at her. And though the rest of the cadre still slept together in twos and threes, Tinnai's place beside her was empty and held no warmth of their leader.

She stirred the black ashes with the point of her pipe. They flaked and rose in nervous flutters upon the warmth of the embers below. These she nursed with gentle puffs of breath that filled the air with a light morning fog that faded away with the heat of the coals. A few pages, torn and placed just so and the flames caught it and curled the paper quickly. She propped a half open book on either side and let the flames lick the pages until they had caught. One more closed book, shoved deep in the coals, would burn long and slow.

With the fire secure, she pulled on the jacket she'd been lying on. It had come from the large boy with the broken knees. Someone else had crushed his windpipe. The coat fell past her own knees and, while it might be a danger in a fight, she loved the extra warmth. She'd take the risk.

The bookstore loomed huge, far bigger than their maintenance shed. The area of the firepit and where they'd slept had once held more bookcases. She could see the markings in the soot and blood-drenched carpet. But the Taka must have burned the shelves as soon as they were empty. This left a space big enough to have a fighting practice with half the cadre at a time. The towering rows of shelves ran toward the front of the store.

A set of stairs exited downward, and last night she'd taken a flaming twist of pages to relock the entrance to the Zenbu tunnels from the inside. Boxes of books were stacked all about the basement. She'd become lost in the wonder of it all until the paper torch had burned her fingers and she'd been plunged into darkness. There were so many books to burn that she'd had a terrible time finding her way back to the basement stairs.

Yet on the main floor, they had burned barely a quarter of the supply. Ri looked up. Two more floors surrounded the hollow center of the store like great balconies. The morning light shone down from above. Bounty beyond belief. It really seemed that there were enough books to burn forever.

She was so intent on the blue walls and soft yellow ceilings embracing thousands upon thousands of multi-colored spines and shining covers, that she'd have fallen over Ninka if not for the hunter's sharp hiss.

"Careful, Ri. You walk like a newborn who has never seen the world before."

Ri rested the end of her pipe on the floor and squatted beside the chief hunter. Ninka's dark eyes remained hidden inside the hood of her parka, which had once been silvered, but had darkened with large splotches of grime and old blood. She sat on the chain which trailed out through the bolt-hole in the door to the ankle of the sacrificial. They'd found a boy who had merely been knocked out, and chained him last night. Who knew what the Zenbu would do if the sacrificial were not offered. But he was still there, his back blocking most of the cold draft through the hole. Warm to his bare back.

"What of the others?"

Ninka looked left and right and pulled back her

hood enough that Ri could see how wide her eyes were.

"All gone."

"All?" They had stacked the bodies of the Taka Cadre outside the store. Many more than they'd first thought. It was a wonder that nineteen Tanchos had killed thirty-two Hawks. They'd thought about putting them through the door in the basement, but the risk was too great even if the other side were unlocked. One did not offer the Zenbu passage and expect to survive.

"Every one." Ninka looked about again. "I heard them," she whispered and retreated back into her hood.

"What did they say? What did they look like?"

"Sss," the hiss sounded again. "You are still a child, Ri. Yes, I crept to the door to hear them, but I could not understand a word. It is said they still speak the old Japanese, that they refused to learn Anglese. But one does not look upon the face of the Zenbu and live. You did well last night, but even you would die should you come face to face with The All."

"But the sacrificial sees—"

"The sacrificial is already dead. The All merely bide their time. I am fourteen and have been hunting four years longer than you. None survive who have seen the Zenbu. So it is said and so it is true."

Ri bowed her forehead to the carpet, the thick dust clogged her nose, but she didn't dare sneeze. One did not argue with elders, especially about such a well known truth as the death that lurked in every Zenbu's eyes. The flush of shame burned at her cheeks. She crawled away backwards to show the abjectness of her apology. Tinnai always said that Ninka was the best. And Ri had questioned their greatest hunter who was far older and far wiser. She even had breasts. Ri had none, still a little girl.

When she had backed out of sight, she stood and turned away. By chance she'd arrived at the bottom of the staircase reaching up to the next floor. Others scouted it last night, while she helped carry out the dead Hawks. The steps climbed forever upward until finally the high ceiling became the floor beneath her feet. More books ranged about the floor. The shelves all full, the Taka had not burned these.

High windows. Tall bookcases barricaded the view. Pressing her face against a crack, she couldn't quite see the sidewalk where they had stacked the bodies, but the litter-strewn street stretched clear and quiet in the morning light. The path she had cleared for their attack had already been partially obscured by leaves and bits of old cloth. Turning back to the room, further exploration revealed a small bathroom with a dry toilet and a shattered sink.

The third floor seemed so far away, but she forced her tired legs to climb this last flight. She must learn the defenses of their new home.

The top floor was but a duplicate of the second.

Towering bookcases cluttered with the colors of the rainbow. She especially liked the ones with silver or gold that reflected the morning light until they sparkled. Where the bathroom had been below, a metal ladder led upward to a roof hatch. A heavy chain and a rusted lock held it securely in place. Many scrapes and dents marked where the Hawks had tried to break the lock without success. Ri preferred it locked.

At the street side of the store, great panels of glass let the pink light of morning shine in. Rather than massive barricades blocking cracked and broken windows, Ri stepped into an alcove wrapped in glass on three sides. The charred hulk of the bank filled the block below. Only one or two buildings remained intact on any city block, the rest were shattered or burned leaving only rubble.

And the rubble had been over-foraged by the survivors of the death of the world. The hunters had to search far and wide to find food. Tales of buildings like the bookstore but with food lining the long shelves were told only late at night in disbelieving whispers.

From her high window, Ri considered the vast plain of ruined buildings that stretched to the horizon and beyond. Were there other hunters out there in the far distance who did not know of the struggles of Tancho Cadre and their triumph over the Taka?

The vista made her wonder for the first time about the vast possibilities of the world before it had died. Could the old vehicles that littered the streets have taken her to strange and wonderful places? Were there once vehicles that flew along the mighty bands of steel that stretched out from the Kintetsu Rail Station where Kintetsu Cadre squatted? Had the street below once been filled with people? What magic lay deep in the tunnels of the Zenbu?

Ri tried to picture it, a huge throng would be needed if the street were to be clogged, but she could not stretch her mind beyond two or perhaps three cadres' hunters carefully avoiding each other as they crept by on opposite sides of the street, pretending the others were not there.

From this bay window she could see almost the entire street, though the sacrificial huddled out of view directly below. Two more windows thrust out from the front of the building. She hurried to the next and nearly fell into Tinnai's lap. Her leader squatted on the floor with a book open in front of her. There were no pictures, just lines of tiny black writing. Her wounded arm in a sling.

"What are you doing, Mother Tinnai?"

"Good morning to you as well, Ri-chan."

Heat flooded her cheeks as she dropped to the floor and bowed her head to the carpet, softer and much cleaner than the one by the entrance.

"It's okay little one. After last night you are no longer a child. It was wrong to call you so."

A gentle hand tipped her back to sitting position.

Tinnai sat bathed in the morning's reds and golds, haloed by the sun now rising over the ruined city. Leaning forward, Ri could indeed see the sacrificial squatting by the door below. From here, a guard could watch the whole street.

"I am reading about a man named Watson. He is looking for a place to live. And a man who is dripping blood from his finger," she pointed her own finger at the book and squinted at it, "a Holmes. They decide to live together."

"A wounded hunter. Do they find it? Do they find the place to live?"

Tinnai flipped the page forward and followed her finger slowly down the page.

"Yes, on a street called Baker."

"Just like us. It is a good story, Mother Tinnai. Are there others?"

She waved her good hand at the towering bookshelves about them. "What did you think those were?"

Ri looked up at the row upon row of towering bookcases. There were not just a few stories there, not even hundreds, there must be millions. Every page might have a story of new homes.

There must be other secrets about homes in these stories. Ways to protect their home. Ways to make the Tancho Cadre safe. And powerful.

"Mother Tinnai, you must teach me to read. You must. Then I can help you save the Tancho and we shall become great and wealthy and rebuild the last city of the world into the great wonder it once was. We shall send people out exploring to build other cities. We will save the hunters there, or send new ones. I must know what is in these books, Mother Tinnai. You must teach me."

Her merry laugh finally stumbled Ri to a halt.

"It would be my honor to teach you, Ri-san of the Great Hope."

Her grown up name. Ri bowed her head to the carpet and tears ran from her eyes and made dark spots on the sun-golden carpet. Ri-san of the Great Hope.

"I will not let you down, Mother Tinnai. I promise. I will never fail the cadre."

*Keep reading at fine retails everywhere.*
*The Nara Reaction*

# ABOUT THE AUTHOR

M.L. Buchman started the first of over 50 novels and even more short stories while flying from South Korea to ride across the Australian Outback. All part of a solo around-the-world bicycle trip (a mid-life crisis on wheels) that ultimately launched his writing career.

Booklist has selected his military and firefighter series(es) as 3-time "Top 10 Romance of the Year." NPR and Barnes & Noble have named other titles "Top 5 Romance of the Year." In 2016 he was a finalist for RWA's RITA award.

He has flown and jumped out of airplanes, can single-hand a fifty-foot sailboat, and has designed and built two houses. In between writing, he also quilts. M.L. is constantly amazed at what can be done with a degree in geophysics. He also writes: contemporary romance, thrillers, and SF. More info at: www.mlbuchman.com

*Join the conversation:*
www.mlbuchman.com

# Other works by M. L. Buchman:

**The Night Stalkers**

MAIN FLIGHT
*The Night Is Mine*
*I Own the Dawn*
*Wait Until Dark*
*Take Over at Midnight*
*Light Up the Night*
*Bring On the Dusk*
*By Break of Day*

WHITE HOUSE HOLIDAY
*Daniel's Christmas*
*Frank's Independence Day*
*Peter's Christmas*
*Zachary's Christmas*
*Roy's Independence Day*
*Damien's Christmas*

AND THE NAVY
*Christmas at Steel Beach*
*Christmas at Peleliu Cove*

5E
*Target of the Heart*
*Target Lock on Love*
*Target of Mine*

**Firehawks**

MAIN FLIGHT
*Pure Heat*
*Full Blaze*
*Hot Point*
*Flash of Fire*
*Wild Fire*

SMOKEJUMPERS
*Wildfire at Dawn*
*Wildfire at Larch Creek*
*Wildfire on the Skagit*

**Delta Force**
*Target Engaged*
*Heart Strike*
*Wild Justice*

**White House Protection Force**
*Off the Leash*
*On Your Mark*
*In the Weeds*

**Where Dreams**
*Where Dreams are Born*
*Where Dreams Reside*
*Where Dreams Are of Christmas*
*Where Dreams Unfold*
*Where Dreams Are Written*

**Eagle Cove**
*Return to Eagle Cove*
*Recipe for Eagle Cove*
*Longing for Eagle Cove*
*Keepsake for Eagle Cove*

**Henderson's Ranch**
*Nathan's Big Sky*
*Big Sky, Loyal Heart*

**Love Abroad**
*Heart of the Cotswolds: England*
*Path of Love: Cinque Terre, Italy*

**Dead Chef Thrillers**
*Swap Out!*
*One Chef!*
*Two Chef!*

**Deities Anonymous**
*Cookbook from Hell: Reheated*
*Saviors 101*

**SF/F Titles**
*The Nara Reaction*
*Monk's Maze*
*the Me and Elsie Chronicles*

**Strategies for Success (NF)**
*Managing Your Inner Artist/Writer*
*Estate Planning for Authors*